Martin Chatterton

STUNT

MONKEYS

FOUR BOYS GO APE!

Stripes

WARNING!

How far can you run with your boots full of custard without spilling a drop?

Do you know the exact number of chickens you can balance on your nose while bouncing on a trampoline?

Or if you can stuff twenty-seven very smelly fish down your underpants inside a minute?

You don't have a clue, do you?

Don't worry. No one in the whole world would know things as weird as that...

No one apart from...

...THE STUNT MONKEYS!

STENCH
Can reach speeds of forty kmph through farting alone. Just make sure you're not standing behind him...

KURTIS
It could be argued that Kurtis is the brains of the group ... which isn't saying much.

GRUNT

The pocket rocket – just point him at the nearest trouble and stand well back. No batteries required.

EINSTEIN

Einstein might look like a genius but this is far from true. He is, however, a master at inventing useless objects.

CHAPTER
ONE

NOBODY EXPECTS
THE GRASS INSPECTORS

It was another dull day in Sludgeville. The Stunt Monkeys were round at Stench's house. Kurtis rubbed a thick patch of grime from Stench's bedroom window and looked outside.

He let out a long sigh. "This has to be the most boring town in the world. If something doesn't happen

soon I'm going to pass out."

Einstein nodded. He adjusted his spectacles and pointed at a block of wood in his hand. "According to my Bore-O-Meter, Sludgeville is the dullest town on the planet."

"Einstein," said Grunt, "that's a block of wood."

"It's my Bore-O-Meter!"

"No, it's a block of—"

"Will you two put a sock in it?" groaned Kurtis. "It's bad enough having to live in Sludgeville without listening to you idiots droning on."

Stench farted in agreement.

"OK, have it your way," said Grunt, grabbing hold of Einstein. "It's a Bore-O-Meter. Either way it's going to disappear right up—"

But before the world could learn exactly where the Bore-O-Meter was going to disappear, there was a screech of tyres from outside.

Grunt was at the window in a flash, dragging Einstein with him.

"Grass Inspectors!" he snarled. "Looks like trouble." The boys crowded round to watch.

A black van skidded to a halt outside the house next door where Verna Smidgeon, Stench's neighbour, was just picking up her newspaper.

A loud, high-pitched, metallic voice boomed out from a speaker mounted on top of the van.

YOU! YES, YOU IN THE DRESSING GOWN! THIS IS THE SLUDGEVILLE COUNCIL GRASS INSPECTION TEAM! YOU ARE IN VIOLATION OF COUNCIL RULE NUMBER 476B! NOW...DROP...THE...NEWSPAPER ...AND...BACK...AWAY...FROM ...THE...GRASS!!!

Mrs Smidgeon let out a squeal of terror. Grass Inspectors! Instantly the van doors crashed open and five large masked men, dressed from head to toe in black combat uniform, leaped out.

"Show time," muttered Kurtis.

Stench farted twice.

"Couldn't agree more, Stenchy," gasped Grunt, fanning the air. "Definitely a two fart situation."

"GO!GO!GO!" screamed the Grass Inspectors as they pounded up the garden path.

"SUSPECT ARMED!" screeched the voice from the van.

"Armed?" said Kurtis as he craned forward for a better look. "She's only holding a newspaper!"

Two of the Inspectors pinned Mrs Smidgeon to the wall, while the

remaining Grass Inspectors dropped to the ground as if expecting to be attacked at any moment. The newspaper was ripped from Mrs Smidgeon's fingers.

"AREA SECURE!" shouted one of the Inspectors.

"Phew," said Grunt from the window. "Now we can all relax!"

There was a moment's silence.

A tall thin man stepped down from the van and held the door open for a small fat man wearing a heavy gold chain round his neck. The chain clanked as the man wobbled down the garden path towards the house.

"Well look who it is," said Kurtis. "Our old friend..."

"Mayor McFoodle!" gasped Mrs Smidgeon. At the sight of Mayor McFoodle Stench let out a low growl (and a particularly stinky fart). The Stunt Monkeys held their noses and watched the action unfold.

"I see you've met my Grass Inspectors, Mrs Smidgeon," said the Mayor. "This is my assistant, Mr Pink."

The tall thin man made a face like he'd just sucked a lemon and nodded icily to Mrs Smidgeon.

Mayor McFoodle looked around Mrs Smidgeon's scruffy little garden.

"Oh dear," he said. "Tut tut, Mrs Smidgeon. This really won't do." He took his steel ruler and placed it upright in the grass.

"Twelve centimetres! Twelve! Really, Mrs Smidgeon, you know better than that."

"But ... but ... I was going to cut it, it's just that m-m-my—"

"Save it for the judge, Smidgeon," said Mayor McFoodle, holding up a pudgy hand. "I've heard it all before: 'I like long grass', 'I'm

growing it for a friend', 'Aliens stole my lawn and replaced it with this longer stuff'. Pah! Sludgeville **Council Rule 476b** clearly states that: No grass is to grow higher than eight centimetres anywhere within the borough of Sludgeville. Eight! Not twelve! It's an open-and-shut case. Now take her away, boys."*

* As the less stupid amongst you may have noticed, Mayor McFoodle is very, very fond of rules. He has a big thick book full of some of the silliest rules you could ever think of (and plenty you couldn't). Just take a look...

Mayor McFoodle's Top Six Rules

Rule 476b

Grass is not allowed to grow taller than eight centimetres. Any grass owner failing to comply will be made to clean the public toilets with their own toothbrush.

Rule 82

No ball games of any kind permitted on council property. No ball games of any kind permitted off council property. No ball games, got it?

Rule 979c

All dogs must wear nappies when in public. Any dog caught pooping on the street will be turned into cat food.

Rule 233e

Chewing gum is strictly prohibited. If you swallow it, it'll wrap around your heart. Don't you know anything?

Rule 904

No balloons, party poppers, tinsel, confetti, streamers, kazoos, horns, whistles or other instrument of celebration may be used in a public place.

Rule 27,676,543,235

Children (nasty little monsters) making any kind of noise on council property will be fed to the council bear.

signed Mayor McFoodle

Up in Stench's bedroom, things were getting heated. Stench had found a particularly rotten, stinky potato and was attempting to hurl it out of the window.

Grunt jumped on him and pinned him to the floor. "Don't do it, Stenchy, it'll just make things worse."

Stench farted angrily and let out a loud wail of frustration.

Mayor McFoodle glanced up at the window. "And don't think I haven't seen you idiots up there. I've got my eye on you lot. If you even so much as think about breaking one of my lovely rules, I'll have you cleaning pigeon poo off the town hall for the rest of your miserable lives!"

He took one last look around the garden. "I don't know, Pink, has everyone forgotten that it's SludgeFest 50 in a matter of weeks? The grass simply must be neat! What would the Grand Sludgemaster say if he saw all these disgusting scruffy lawns?"

"They don't understand, Your Magnificence," sighed Pink, patting Mayor McFoodle on the shoulder.

"Make sure this, this filthy ... weed is cut back, Pink! All of it!"

"Of course," nodded Pink.

With a disgusted wrinkle of his chubby nose, Mayor McFoodle hopped back into the Grass Inspection van and it zipped away in a cloud of dust.

IS YOUR TOWN AS DULL AS A BEIGE CUSHION LEFT OUT IN THE RAIN?

DO YOU FEEL LIKE YOU WANT TO SCREAM?

DOES EVERY DAY FEEL LIKE SUNDAY?

ARE ALL THE SKIES CLOUDY AND GREY?

Then discover where your town rates on the Official Stunt Monkeys Bore-O-Meter*! Just feed in any information about your town that might spell B.O.R.E.D.O.M: a large population of wrinklies, shops that sell slippers or comfy shoes, a Museum of Cheese-Making or Lawn Mowers, total lack of movie theatres … and the Bore-O-Meter* does the rest!

AMAZE your friends when they find out there are duller places than YOUR town!**

THRILL as you compare towns in your area for utter dullness!

FALL ASLEEP when you realize that you have ABSOLUTELY NOTHING TO DO once you've finished finding out just how boring your town really is!

The Bore-O-Meter* comes in two attractive finishes: Raw Pine and Worn Mahogany. Looks just like a lump of wood!***

*Every Bore-O-Meter comes with a completely worthless guarantee!
**Unless you live in Sludgeville or surrounding areas.
***Is, in fact, a lump of wood.
Not to be used while moving.
Suitable for ages 3 and up.

CHAPTER TWO

THE BOOK

Back in Stench's bedroom, the boys were still wrestling with Stench.

"He's gone, Stenchoid," said Kurtis, trying to prise the spud out of Stench's grimy fingers. "C'mon, let go."

"Nerrrk! Grrrrrnnnnch! Shmmmbll!" growled Stench thrashing around wildly.

"Stenchy! Listen! Kurtis is right," said Einstein. "If McFoodle had caught you, he might have got the Clean-Up Squad in and made you..."

"...Tidy your room!" Grunt shouted, grappling with Stench's legs.

Stench stopped struggling immediately, shocked right down to his grubby boxers by the dreadful thought. His room hadn't been tidied since his mother had found a raccoon nesting in his underwear drawer. Reluctantly he released the potato and stomped over into a corner to sulk and think hard about something nice, like burying McFoodle up to his neck in the desert and leaving him for the ants.

Kurtis, Grunt and Einstein sank back exhausted on the floor.

"Man, I hate that McFoodle," said Grunt. "Always sticking his fat nose in where it's not wanted. Someone needs to teach him a lesson!"

"I don't know," said Einstein. "Those Grass Inspectors look pretty nasty to me."

Grunt threw the Bore-O-Meter at him. "You dipstick, Einstein!"

Just then Tim, Stench's mangy-looking pet vulture, flapped up on to the wardrobe to finish off what was left of a tasty, flattened rat that he'd found on the road. A vulture-poo-stained copy of *The Daily Sludge* that had been lining his cage fluttered down on to Kurtis's head.

"Oh great," said Kurtis. "Just what I needed to round the morning off." He scrunched the newspaper up and was about to throw it in a corner when an advert caught his eye...

Coming Soon!
SludgeFest 50!

It's back! And this time it's slightly bigger than last time!

The must-see event of the Sludgeing year,

SludgeFest 50 is coming to Sludgeville on July 13th!!

See: quite interesting displays of sludge!

See: moderately-skilful sludge sculptures!

See: not-boring-at-all sludge technology!

Meet other sludge enthusiasts from around the Sludgeing world!

Also: Sludgeberry Shake competition!

Sludge Idol! Sludge-a-thon!

Morris Dancing display by Ye Merrie Olde Sludgemen!

And your chance to have your photo taken with the

Sludgefest 50 Princesses in their very sparkly dresses!

Get prepared for something nifty,

Come on down to **SludgeFest 50!**

...needed
wanted
...stache.
...consider
...d swap.

Penguin wranglers wanted

The sudden and unexplained rise in the number of illegal penguins entering Sludgeville means that the council are looking for experienced penguin wranglers. Individuals with large hands perferred.

by Horace Cope

SLUDGEscope

LEO
It's time to show off your roar today.

LIBRA
Certain things on your mind – weigh up what they mean.

GEMINI
You'll see things from two sides today. It's time to show off.

PISCES
Things might seem fishy to you today but don't worry - it'll all come clear tomorrow.

TAURUS
Todays' not the day to act like a bull in a china shop…Take it easy!

SCORPIO
Use that sting in your tail to show people what you're really made of - ouch!

For an indepth analysis text mug to 0000.
Each text costs just £9.99

Airborne Special Forces
Council Parking Attendant

Seeking individuals who love really mundane pointless laws to regulate the rising number of penguins being greased in your local area. Stunt Monkeys and time wasters need not apply.

Enrol at Sludgeville College!
Do you feel your lack of sludge knowledge is holding you back? Enrol now for a two year degree in Sludgeonomics and watch your career take off!

"Have you seen this?" said Kurtis, pointing at the newspaper.

"Why are you so interested?" asked Grunt. "It's just the dumb ole SludgeFest. Same rubbish every year. Loads of boring speeches, lots of Sludge-type zombies crowding up the place; you know what it's like."

But Kurtis wasn't listening. A small idea had begun to form in his head.

"Maybe it's time to get The Book out again," he said, "and give McFoodle a few surprises."

There was a long pause during which you could have heard a pin drop. Einstein actually dropped a pin to check and they all heard it loud and clear.

The Stunt Monkeys looked at each other in a meaningful way.

The Book!

Grunt looked at Kurtis and nodded.

"OK, let's do it."

"Do you really think we should?" asked Einstein. "I mean, remember what happened last time with the snails?"

Grunt rolled his eyes and gave Einstein a wedgie to shut him up. Farting quietly with excitement, Stench pulled out a large golden

book from under his bed. He brushed a lump of egg off the cover and placed it on the floor...

The Stunt Monkeys had discovered **The League Of Unbelievable and Amazing World Records** book last year. It was a fantastic book stuffed full of lots of incredible things that people had done to claim a World Record.

The Stunt Monkeys weren't called the Stunt Monkeys back then, of course. That came after they'd decided that weird stunts and record-breaking were just what Sludgeville needed to liven it up. And it seemed that you could get a World Record for just about anything. A few Stunt Monkey favourites:

The League of Unbelievable and Amazing World Records

LEE REDMOND (USA)
World Record for the L o n g e s t Fingernails for a
Female (7 m 51.3 cms). Lee hasn't cut her fingernails
since 1979!

RUDY HORN (GERMANY)
World Record For Catching Teacups on the Head
while Riding a Unicycle – six cups and six saucers
(and a teaspoon and a lump of sugar!) at the
Bertram Mills Circus at Olympia, London, UK 1952

LUCKY DIAMOND RICH (AUSTRALIA)
World Record for the Most Tattooed Human
100% of his body covered in black ink – Lucky has
spent over 1,000 hours having his body tattooed

STEVE URNER (USA)
World Record for the Furthest Cow Pat Toss
81.1m – thrown at the Mountain Festival,
Tehachapi, California, USA on 14 August 1981

ARCHIE
(TRAINED BY CARL BRANHAM UK)
World Record for the Fastest Snail
33cm in two minutes 20 seconds –
sprinted to the winning post at the annual World Snail
Racing Championships held in July 1995 at
Congham, Norfolk, UK

JACK BIBBY (USA)
World Record for Holding the
Most Live Rattlesnakes in the
Mouth by their Tails –
ten rattlesnakes in his mouth for
ten seconds on 9th November
2006 in New York City, USA

Things had been going pretty well for the boys until they'd tried snail racing. During an attempt on the **World Record For Snail Racing** behind Le Sludge, Sludgeville's snootiest restaurant, several of the faster competitors had escaped and ended up in Mrs McFoodle's salad. Mrs McFoodle had barfed all over Mayor McFoodle and a visiting team of Japanese Sludge Inspectors. Things got awfully messy.

Ever since then, Mayor McFoodle
had had his eye on the Stunt
Monkeys and had put a stranglehold
on all fun in Sludgeville. More and
more rules were introduced. More
teams of inspectors had been
recruited. The Stunt Monkeys had
decided to lay low for a while, and
**The League Of Unbelievable and
Amazing World Records** had been
put away.

Until now...

The boys gathered round and
looked at The Book. Just seeing it
again sent a tingle of excitement
down all four spines in the room. All
except for Tim's spine because
vulture spines only tingle at the sight

of something dead or, possibly, very old people.

"You know what I say?" said Kurtis. "Stuff McFoodle and his stupid rules! I think it's time the Stunt Monkeys came out of retirement!"

CHAPTER
THREE

UNDERPANTS SHMUNDERPANTS

The Stunt Monkeys wasted no time in getting started.

First they called **The League Of Unbelievable and Amazing World Records**, who sent a nice lady called Miss Axelsen down from Grotburg to see what they could do.

Stench kicked off with an attempt

to beat the **World Record for Stuffing Kippers Down Your Underpants**. At 6 a.m. on the fields behind Sludgeville High, he stuffed twenty-seven extremely smelly smoked fish down his pants in less than a minute. Einstein, as usual, was making sure everything met the standards required – counting the fish into Stench's pants and checking that none slipped out.

"Remarkable!" said Miss Axelsen, adjusting the clothes peg on her nose and scribbling in her notebook. She put on a surgical rubber glove and shook Stench's hand.

"Congratula—," she began, before
a triumphant high-pitched voice cut
across her.

"Stop right there, you vile little
sneaks! Up to your nasty tricks
again, I see!" yelled Mayor
McFoodle, springing up from
beneath a secret trapdoor cunningly
disguised as a drain cover. A gang
of vicious-looking Ninja Traffic
Wardens bounced up right behind

him and stood glaring at the Stunt
Monkeys through the slits in their
ninja hoods. Mayor McFoodle was
still wearing his pyjamas, and a
strange-looking electronic hat that
beeped and gave off little blue
electric sparks.

"How did you know?" blurted Einstein. "Shouldn't you still be asleep?"

McFoodle pointed at his weird hat and smiled.

"Never underestimate Horace T. McFoodle! This hat is an Odd Behaviour Detection Device, designed by Sludgeville's brainiest council scientists. Since that episode with the snails I never sleep without it and it alerted me instantly to your jiggery-pokery. You are breaking Sludgeville **Council Rule 276: No food to be eaten on council property!**"

"But he's not eating them!" pointed out Kurtis. "He's stuffing them down his underpants!"

Mayor McFoodle waved a hand airily.

"Eating shmeating, underpants shmunderpants, it's still against my ... I mean *council* rules! **Rule 276** covers all mishandling of food. Besides, you're being cruel to the kippers."

"But the kippers are already dead!" yelled Kurtis.

Mayor McFoodle's eyes narrowed dangerously.

"So now you're admitting you killed those poor creatures?"

Grunt looked like he was about to explode. Mayor McFoodle raised his hand and the Ninja Traffic Wardens slid forward like one of Stench's specials. Silent but deadly.

44

"Oh dear," said Miss Axelsen. "I'm afraid your record won't be official. **The League Of Unbelievable and Amazing World Records** can't do anything illegal, you know."

"She's right," grinned McFoodle. "Rules is rules! And don't ever forget who's in charge round here!" he hissed, before whizzing off in the official Sludgeville Council hovercraft, driven by Assistant Pink.

Later that day, down by a deserted part of the canal, Grunt tried to beat the **World Record For Balancing Chickens On Your Head**.

Mayor McFoodle was nowhere to be seen.

Einstein had checked the area for concealed trapdoors, secret passageways and sneaky hidey-holes with a special Anti-McFoodle scanner he was trying out. There weren't even any nearby handy trees or hills to hide behind.

The only sound

46

came from a few small bubbles popping gently on the surface of the canal.

The coast was clear.

"Magnificent!" said Miss Axelsen, watching Grunt hoisting one last chicken on to his head. "That's the most amazing chicken balancing stunt I've ever seen! You've just broken a World Record!"

She scribbled something in her book and reached out to shake Grunt's hand.

47

As she did so, a bright yellow mini-submarine splashed up from the canal in a gigantic plume of murky water and rusted shopping trollies. No sooner had it settled than the hatch flew open and Mayor McFoodle squeezed up into view.

"Stop right there!" he shouted. "This record attempt is against Sludgeville **Council Rule 11,23,483:** No chicken balancing in public!"

"Oh dear," said Miss Axelsen.

"That's not a real rule!" said Einstein. "You've just made that up!"

"Prove it!" said Mayor McFoodle as a posse of Grass Inspectors emerged from the submarine, cracking their knuckles and growling softly.

"Margarine."

Kurtis held out his hand and Einstein handed him a slab of margarine.

"Margarine, check," said Einstein.

"Penguin."

"Penguin, check."

Einstein passed over the last penguin to Kurtis who began spreading margarine on the bird.

"Nerk!" squawked the penguin. "Nerk! Nerk!"

It was the final penguin needed to break the **World Record For Combined Speed Penguin Car Stuffing**. Anyone who knows anything about Speed

Penguin Stuffing knows that you
need properly greased penguins to
stand any chance of getting forty-
seven of them inside a small family
car (which had been kindly supplied
by Miss Axelsen, who was looking a
bit worried about all that margarine
staining her upholstery).

"Nerk! Nerk! Nerk! Nerk! Nerk!
Nerk! Nerk!" squawked the
penguins. "Nerk! Nerk! Nerk! Nerk!
Nerk!"

Kurtis, the last slippery bird tucked
under his arm, paused and looked
around slowly. They were miles from
town, almost near Grotburg, way,
way out on the edge of Sludgeville
swamp. Nobody ever came out
here.

Not even Horace T. McFoodle.

Kurtis leaned forward to ease the
penguin into place when, with a
deafening clatter of whirring
helicopter blades, the Council SWAT
team helicopter roared out from
behind some low clouds.

In a flash, an Airborne Special
Forces Council Parking Attendant
dived down and swiped the bird
right out of Kurtis's hands.

Mayor McFoodle leaned out of the helicopter window.

"**RULE 43**!" he shouted above the engine noise. "**NO UNAUTHORIZED PUBLIC PENGUIN GREASING! NOW GET THOSE PENGUINS BACK TO SLUDGEVILLE ZOO RIGHT AWAY!**"

Miss Axelsen put her notebook away.

"I'M SORRY, BOYS," she yelled as she pulled greasy penguins out of her car. "CALL ME WHEN YOU HAVE SOMETHING YOU *ARE* ALLOWED TO DO!"

Sliding around on her seat she started the engine and zipped off back to **The League Of Unbelievable and Amazing World Records** office.

Mayor McFoodle watched her go,
a satisfied smile on his ugly face.

"RULES IS RULES," he yelled,
tapping a thick book of Sludgeville
Council Rules. "GET USED TO IT,
YOU IDIOTS! NOTHING, AND I
MEAN NOTHING, IS GOING TO
INTERFERE WITH SLUDGEFEST 50!"

CHAPTER
FOUR

I WANNA DUCKY!

Back in Stench's bedroom, Kurtis
picked up The Book. "One more," he
said. "Let's just try one last stunt."

"Yeah," said Grunt. He grabbed
Einstein in a friendly headlock and
rubbed his knuckles playfully across
his scalp. "McFoodle isn't going to
beat the Stunt Monkeys, right?"

"Mumblebumblegumble," agreed Stench, absent-mindedly pulling a fish from his underwear.

"C'mon, Einstein," said Kurtis. "We'll pick something really simple, something safe. Something where absolutely nothing can go wrong."

"OK, OK," said Einstein, holding his hands up in surrender. "One more then."

Kurtis grinned and began flicking through the book. He turned a page and stopped.

"I've got a good one," he said. "It can't fail!"

"What?" said Grunt.

"Balloon-folding," said Kurtis, "you know, making funny animals and stuff out of balloons! What could go wrong with that?"

The attempt on the **World Record For Speed Balloon Folding** started promisingly. Kurtis found a super-large box of balloons at Stunt Monkeys HQ (otherwise known as his dad's garage, which was always full of useful and interesting objects including balloons, and helium and some showroom dummies that could possibly be important later on in the story).

The boys picked a very quiet spot
on the edge of the Sludge Industries
factory between the two stinking
sludge storage towers.

"Yeuch!" said Kurtis, holding his
nose as they approached the towers.
"I reckon this place is too smelly
even for McFoodle!"

"Never mind McFoodle," gasped
Einstein holding his T-shirt up to his
nose. "What about us?"

"We hang out with Stench,"
gasped Grunt. "We're used to it."

They got to the top of the hill and
stopped.

"Oh no," said Einstein. "Look."

Right under the towers a small group of itsy-bitsy-teeny-tiny-eeny-weeny kids stood in the drizzle playing whatever games itsy-bitsy-teeny-tiny-eeny-weeny kids play.

One of them was a small spotty kid who looked like a young warthog.

Horace McFoodle Junior.

Son of Mayor McFoodle.

"That's it," said Einstein, starting back down the hill. "I'm out of here."

"Wait!" said Kurtis. "This could be a good thing."

Einstein stopped and stared at him. "How? How could this possibly be a good thing?"

"Well," said Kurtis. "Say we do get young Horace involved in this stunt and say Mayor McFoodle does happen to catch us doing it..."

"...then how's he going to say anything when Horace Junior is doing it too?" chimed in Grunt. "Kurtis, you're a genius!"

"Well I don't like to boast but..."

Even Einstein had to admit it was a good plan.

The only trouble was Horace. He was, like his father, a complete twerp.

"I wanna ducky balloon!" said Horace. "Horace wanna hold a ducky! You said I could hold a ducky!"

"Yeah yeah, kid," said Kurtis. "You can have a ducky when Einstein here's worked out how to make a ducky, OK? Now stand back; give us some room to work! You getting anywhere yet, Einstein?"

"I'm doing my best!" said Einstein. "It's harder than it looks."

The balloons were proving difficult to inflate until Grunt found some helium at the bottom of the balloon box. Before you could say "hiss" there were a large number of balloons tied to the fence waiting to be folded. At that moment a Sludge Industries guard came round the corner.

"Oi! You lot! What do you think you're doing?" he yelled.

"Quick!" said Grunt to the tinies. "Grab as many balloons as you can and meet us by the school!"

Four or five kids grabbed hold of the balloons...

...and floated straight up into the grey Sludgeville sky.

Horace McFoodle Junior looked down, a surprised expression on his face as he drifted upwards.

"Daddy's not going to like thiiiiiiiiiiiiiiiiisssssss!" he wailed, before the breeze whisked him away. Soon all that could be seen of Horace was a dot in the distance, and then ... nothing.

"That's blown it," said Kurtis, as they ran from the security guard.

"Whoo-ee!" said Grunt, turning his head to watch. "Look at them go!"

"Mumblemumblemumble!" mumbled Stench, which roughly translated as: "Where do you think they're going to land?"

"Hmm," said Einstein, tapping away on his calculator. "According to this they are headed straight for..."

SOMEWHERE ABOVE ALASKA

SUNDAY, 11.27 A.M.

"Uh, Anchorage 211, this is DC flight 107 out of Detroit calling Anchorage chzzz. Come in, Anchorage 211, we have a, um chzzz-crackle ... problem. Out."

"Roger, DC107. Chzzz-crackle Anchorage control reading you loud and clear chzzz. Go ahead. Out. Chzzz."

"Roger, Anchorage. Um ... we have an unidentified bogey approx chzzz-crackle five miles north-east. Out."

"Roger. Suggest chzzz you clean your nose next time you fly DC107 – hur, hur,

hur. Out. Chzzz-click."

"Roger. Har-de-har har. Yes, yes, very chzzz-crackle amusing, Anchorage. Now what do we do about this bogey? Out."

"Roger. Sorry, DC107, we have a negative, repeat negative on any bogey in your area. You are chzzz-crackle flashing up clear and strong and solo at 28,000 feet. No aircraft in your flight corridor. Chzzz Out."

"Roger, Anchorage, chzzz but this is no aircraft. It's getting closer ...
oh my goodness! It's a..."

CHAPTER
FIVE

KOREA CALLING

Assistant Pink nervously tapped on the door.

"Cough."

The Boss wasn't going to like this.

"Cough-cough."

"What now, Pink?" barked Mayor McFoodle. He was sitting behind his big desk holding two phones and

looking at a computer screen. "Can't you see I'm busy trying to find poor little Horace? I've got the Coastguard on line one and the Grand Sludgemaster himself on line two! Not to mention Mrs McFoodle on hold on line three ... and Mrs McFoodle does not like to be kept waiting!"

"Very sorry, Your Most Glorious Fantasticness, but I think you may need to speak to this caller. He says he's from the Korean Air Force."

"The what?"

Mayor McFoodle snatched the phone out of Assistant Pink's hand.

"Yes, yes? Who is this? What business do you have with me? I'm a very important person indeed and I am extremely busy trying to find my son. Now, be quick!"

BUT THIS OBJECT SEEM TO BELONG YOU WHEN WE CHECKED PHOTO FROM SPY PLANE WE SENT TO INVESTIGATE.

BELONG ME? WHAT BELONG ME? I MEAN, BELONGS TO ME? WHAT ARE YOU TALKING ABOUT, COLONEL?

OBJECT IN SKY IS HORACE JUNIOR. YOUR SON, MR FOODLE. HOLDING BIG LOTS OF BALLOON.

HORACE? WHAT'S HORACE JUNIOR DOING FLOATING OVER KOREA? HE DOESN'T EVEN KNOW WHERE IT IS! IT CAN'T BE HIM!

There was a pause in the conversation.

SO OK WE SHOOT?

JUMPING JELLYFISH! NO, NO, NO, COLONEL SUNG! NOT OK YOU SHOOT! MRS MCFOODLE WOULD DO HER NUT! JUST GET HIM DOWN SAFELY AND I'LL WORK IT ALL OUT WITH YOU.

OKEY-DOKEY MR FOODLE. WE JUST SHOOT SOME BALLOON, YES? MAKE HIM DROP, BUT SLOW MAYBE. HE IN LOT OF TROUBLE. MAYBE STAY HERE FOR LONG TIME. COULD BE JAIL MAYBE.

JAIL?

Mayor McFoodle hung up.

There was only one possible explanation for poor Horace's balloon flight – those stupid Stunt Monkeys had been up to their tricks again. He snapped an official SludgeFest 50 souvenir pencil in fury. Well this time they'd gone too far! Mayor Horace T. McFoodle had had about all he could take of those idiotic boys. It was time for action!

"Pink!" he barked. "Call an emergency meeting! We've got work to do!"

CHAPTER
SIX

THE TERMINATOR

By that evening Mayor McFoodle
had his emergency plan all worked
out. The Stunt Monkeys were in for
the shock of their miserable little
lives!

The whole of Sludgeville had
squeezed into the Town Hall for the
Extraordinary Emergency Meeting.

The place was packed. The Stunt
Monkeys sat at the front of the stage
as Mayor McFoodle explained their
latest trick.

"North Korea?" everyone gasped.
Mayor McFoodle nodded grimly as
he pointed with a long stick at a
map of the world.

"North flaming Korea!"

Einstein noticed that he was actually pointing at southern Sweden, but decided that now probably wasn't a good time to mention it.

"Your idiot children have sent my Horace to North Korea!" said Mayor McFoodle. "North Korea!"

He glared at the Stunt Monkeys and their parents, who sat in the front row shuffling their feet.

"And four more kids all over the place!"

Mayor McFoodle flicked his pointy stick up at the map again.

"Emily Gurning. Landed on the CN Tower in Toronto. Chet Frimpling. Caused a flight out of Anchorage to

divert to Russia. Bonnie-Rae Tootleshtump. Landed in a snake-infested swamp in Bulawayo. And poor Sunil Patel was blasted high into the stratosphere after drifting across a powerful steam geyser in Iceland. Last seen over northern Finland."

There was a wail from Mrs Patel.

"Need I go on?" said Mayor McFoodle.

He mopped his brow, handed the pointer to Assistant Pink and stared grimly at the Stunt Monkeys before addressing the audience.

"This tomfoolery has to be stopped! I shouldn't have to remind you that SludgeFest 50 is right here in Sludgeville, in less than five weeks! We need action against these hooligans and I know exactly what needs to be done!"

Mayor McFoodle nodded towards the back of the hall. "Mr Pink, show our guest in if you please."

Assistant Pink opened the door at the back of the room.

Through it stepped the biggest man ever seen in Sludgeville, a solid slab of hard muscle and bone, wearing an army-style uniform. He was as neat as a crisp new banknote.

His belt shimmered with polish.

His boots shone like black diamonds.

His eyes were hidden behind mirrored sunglasses.

He glared around the room and marched towards the desk, his heels thumping against the tiles, the floor shaking. Some smaller children screamed and one nervy woman fainted.

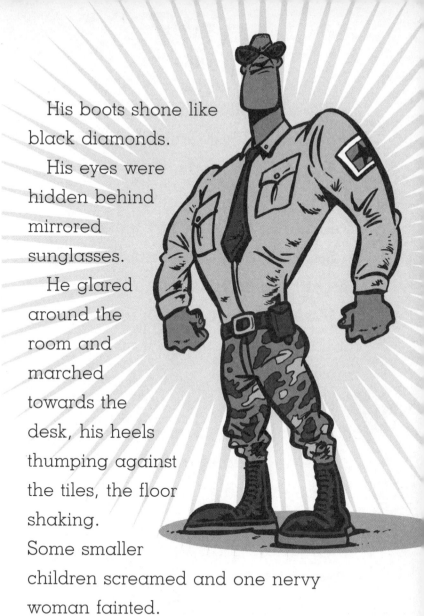

"Good grief!" said Einstein, grabbing hold of Grunt's arm. "Look at the size of that guy!"

"I've got a bad feeling about this," said Kurtis. "A very bad feeling."

Stench made a little noise, which might have been a laugh but wasn't.

"Doesn't look so tough to me," said Grunt, but you could tell he didn't mean it.

Reaching the front of the hall the big man swung to attention, stamped his heels together and screamed at Mayor McFoodle in a voice that sounded like a jet plane making an emergency landing on a sheet of glass.

"SERGEANT BONES, SIR!

REEEEEEEEEE-PORTING-AH FOR DUTY, SIR!"

"Hmm, yes, right. Um, very good, Sergeant," said Mayor McFoodle. "Please stand at, um, ease."

"THANK YOU-AH, SIR!" screeched Sergeant Bones. He slammed his feet about 30 centimetres apart. "STANDING-AH AT-AH EEEEEEEEEEEEEEASE-AH, SIR!"

The Mayor turned to the Stunt Monkeys' parents with a sly smile.

"This is Sergeant James 'The Terminator' Bones. He will be looking after your children for the next month. Tell them what it is you do, Sergeant."

"YES-AH, SIR! THANK YOU, SIR!" The Sergeant slowly swivelled his granite head towards the audience, the lights bouncing off his sunglasses.

"I RUN THE JAMES T. BONES BOOT CAMP FOR NASTY BRATS OUT IN THE MIDDLE OF ABSOLUTELY-AH NOWHERE!" he bellowed. "IT'SAMONTHOFONE HUNNERDPERCENTSHEERHELL ONEARTHGUARANTEEDTOCURE ANYFOOLBOYWHOGETSTOOSASSY

ANSWERSBACKSHOWSDISRESPEK'
OROTHERWISEGETSTOODAMNBIG
FORHISBOOTS!ANYQUESTIONS-AH?"

There was stunned silence in the
hall. The Stunt Monkeys looked as
though they'd been hit by a tornado.
Stench farted softly.

"I'd like to say his bark is
worse than his bite," smiled
Mayor McFoodle holding his
palms out. "But I'd be lying."

"Boot Camp?" said Kurtis's
mum, Doreen Dipstick. "My child
isn't going there! It sounds terrible!"

Don Dipstick agreed. Boot Camp
sounded too nasty for words.

Grunt, Stench and Einstein's
parents chimed in, all agreeing that

none of their children would be
going anywhere near Sergeant
Bones's terrible camp, bad
behaviour or no bad behaviour.

"In that case," said Mayor
McFoodle, nodding towards the
Sludgeville Chief of Police, Spud
O'Really, "we have no option but to
sling 'em all in jail until they're thirty
years old."

"Boot Camp it is then," said Grunt.

"Parp," farted Stench, which
seemed to sum it up.

"There is one other, titchy detail I
should mention," said Mayor
McFoodle, fixing the Stunt Monkeys
with a beady stare. "The upcoming
SludgeFest needs four SludgeFest

Princesses to
carry the Grand
Sludgemaster's
golden robe. As
you know this is a
very great honour,
usually given to
Sludgeville's
four prettiest
young ladies.
However, this
year, so I can
keep an eye
on them at
all times, the
SludgeFest
Princesses will
be ... you four!"

He pointed at the Stunt Monkeys.

There was a gasp from the audience.

Mayor McFoodle smirked. "I'm told the dresses are particularly sparkly this year. Lots of frills. Very pink."

For once Kurtis was lost for words. Einstein looked like he was going to be sick.

It was hard to tell what Stench thought. He was grinding his teeth so hard it sounded like thunder. Grunt coughed and turned pale. The thought of becoming a SludgeFest Princess was causing his brain to short circuit. With a soft moan he fainted and everything went black...

GRUNT'S MAD STUNTS!

Hi, lovely readers! Stunt Monkey fans always ask me: Grunt, O Glorious One, do you have any handy Magnificent Stunt Monkey tips to pass along? So here they are:

When attempting anything remotely dangerous make sure you have a video camera handy! TV companies pay good money to see you fall flat on your face, dude! Oh, and wear lots of helmets, pads, that kind of stuff.

Only trained Magnificent Stunt Monkeys personnel should try certain of my favourite records. I'm thinking particularly of Speed Lion-Tail Knotting, Freestyle Gorilla Wrestling and Human Pinball On Ice.

PS Not everyone is cut out for the Krazee World of Record-Breaking!

CHAPTER
SEVEN

AN UNFORTUNATE INCIDENT AT SHARK LAKE

At dawn the next morning, the Stunt
Monkeys found themselves far, far
from Sludgeville, a long way past
Grotburg, miles out in the dusty,
deserted desert. The boys stood in
a ragged line rubbing sleepy eyes.
Sergeant Bones, holding his pet
poodle, Snookums, close to his

massive chest, had been yelling at them non-stop for thirty-two very noisy minutes. The poodle didn't seem to notice. Maybe it was deaf, thought Kurtis.

"ASFARASYOUSCUMARE CONCERNED, MYNAMEISSIR!" he screamed.

"Do you know what he's saying?" whispered Grunt to Kurtis.

Kurtis shook his head.

"No clue, Grunt. I think he's just sort of ... shouting."

Sergeant Bones stepped forward and looked down at the boys like they were a bunch of nasty bugs he'd found underneath a stone. "NOWMOVEYOURSORRYLITTLE-

ASSESANDGETINTOTHEGYM!WE
GOTALOTOFWORKTODO!"

He pointed with a stick at a big
shed-style building, screamed
something nasty about their mothers

and followed the Stunt Monkeys into the gym.

Inside, ropes hung from the ceiling and ladders ran up and down the walls.

Sergeant Bones made the Stunt Monkeys climb the ropes and run up and down the ladders and generally tire themselves out.

Then he made them do it all over again.

Then again.

And then one more time for good luck.

And then one more time after that for bad luck.

And one time just because he felt like it.

And one last time because it was a Thursday.

93

"That'll settle the little slimeballs, won't it, Snookums?" said Sergeant Bones.

He was right.

At the end of the first day the little slimeballs got back to the dorm, collapsed into their beds and fell dead asleep.

What seemed like fifteen minutes later – because it was fifteen minutes later – Sergeant Bones yanked them all out of bed and made them paint every green wall in the camp white ... using their tongues.

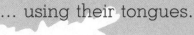

Once the Stunt Monkeys had done that, Sergeant Bones made them paint all the white walls green. The boys painted walls with their tongues all day and then fell sound asleep, exhausted once more. And with very sore tongues.

"Piddy Mith Axthelthen ithn't here to chedd the World Vecord For Tongue Painding," said Kurtis.

By the end of the first week Kurtis, Grunt, Einstein and Stench felt like they were going to die.

By the end of the second week they felt like they wanted to die.

It was time to Do Something.

"It'th time to do thomething," whispered Kurtis one night just after lights out. "We'll be dead before the month'th out if it goeth on like thith. Pluth we'll have no tongueth left."

"If all I've got to look forward to ith wearing a thpangly dress and being Printheth ThludgeFest then I want to die," moaned Grunt. "The thame of it!"

Stench farted in agreement.

"No one'th going to be Printheth ThludgeFest, none of uth anyway, not if I can help it," said Kurtis. "But firtht we have to deal with Captain Buttface out there. Gather round. I've got a cunning plan..."

💀   💀   💀

The next day dawned and, as usual, Sergeant Bones had something extra-nasty planned for the Stunt Monkeys.

"AH'VEBEENTHINKINGTHATAH'VE BEENWAYTOOSOFTWITHYOULITTLE SCUZZBUCKETS!" he screamed. "SO TODAYAH'MGONNASHOWYOUTHE REALMEANINGOFSUFFERING!"

Sergeant Bones jogged them over to a section of Boot Camp they'd never seen before. A pale green, sickly mist drifted across a bug-infested, oozing swamp. In the middle was an obstacle course made up of foul-smelling mudpits, dark underwater tunnels, death slides, spiky tangles of barbed wire and all kinds of extremely nasty-looking stuff.

Einstein moaned softly and looked like he was going to pass out. Kurtis jabbed him in the ribs with an elbow.

"Remember the plan!" he hissed out of the side of his mouth. He winked to the rest of the boys. "We keep smiling. No matter what happens we grin like maniacs and ask for more, right?"

"Check," said Grunt, winking.

Einstein stood up straight and Stench gave the thumbs up.

"LADIESAHWANTYOUTOMEET 'THE SHREDDER'!!" shouted Sergeant Bones.

He chuckled to himself, and fed Snookums with doggy treats as the Stunt Monkeys made their way to the

top of the death slide, the first part of
The Shredder. This wasn't your usual
fun kind of death slide – it was 200m
and ten seconds of sheer terror,
ending in a pit full of worms.

Grunt went first.
"Whoo-hoo!" he yelled,
sliding down and hitting
the muddy floor with a
thump. He spat out a mouthful of
worms. "That was fantastic! Can I go
again, Sarge, please?" he yelled.

Behind his mirrored sunglasses
Sergeant Bones's eyes twitched like
a lizard on a hot rock.

Kurtis, Einstein and Stench all
followed Grunt down the death slide
with big smiles and lots of "whoo-hoos".

This time Sergeant Bones's mouth twitched and a careful listener would have heard the grinding of his massive teeth.

The Shredder was not supposed to be fun.

No matter, thought Sergeant Bones. The Mudpit will sort them out. It always did.

The Mudpit was a disgusting, shallow, thirty-metre long strip of repulsive slime and filth, which lay under a carpet of evil-looking barbed wire. The barbed wire meant that you had to wriggle face down in

the mud to get to the other side.
Sergeant Bones pushed the Stunt
Monkeys in and waited. He knew for
a fact (because he had personally
placed the ingredients in there) that
the mud contained forty buckets of
chopped-up worms, two thousand
rotten fish heads, a bottle of snake
vomit, thirty-three dozen stale eggs,
four hundred litres of rancid ditch
water, a smidgeon of decayed rat
intestines, several large lumps of
cow poo, a sprinkling of cockroach
corpses, and a good dollop of old
lady teacher's earwax.

Einstein slid smoothly through the unspeakable gunge like an oiled otter, popped up on the other side and smiled happily through a face full of mud.

"Man, you got to try that!" he yelled. "Can I have another go, Sarge?"

Grunt, Stench and Kurtis sploshed in and slithered across. They were smiling so much they looked like synchronized mud-swimmers.

"What's next, Sarge?" asked Kurtis. "Is it going to be as much fun as The Mudpit?"

Sergeant Bones turned purple. This

was not supposed to be fun.

After The Mudpit, the Stunt Monkeys laughed like loons along The High-Wire of Hell, grinned like gibbons as they shimmied up The Burning Rope of Misery, slipped through The Pipe of Fear with a carefree chuckle and tittered their way up and over The Wall of Vileness.

"STOP!" screeched Sergeant Bones, his face a purple mask of fury. He put Snookums down and stalked across to the Stunt Monkeys.

"IGOTSOMETHIN'THAT'LLWIPE THOSESMILESOFFYOURFOOL FACES!" he bellowed. "AQUICKDIP INSHARKLAKE!"

The Stunt Monkeys had stuck to the plan all day long and it seemed to be working. Sergeant Bones was definitely beginning to crack. But now, standing on the jetty of Shark Lake, they were starting to wonder.

"I don't know if I can keep this up much longer," hissed Einstein through a fixed grin as Sergeant Bones got a small rowing boat ready at the end of the jetty. "I mean, you can't just smile while a shark's chewing your kneecaps off, can you?!"

Stench farted nervously. Einstein had a point.

Grunt was fiddling with a gigantic piece of elastic rope he'd found coiled up on the jetty. He wrapped it around a couple of the wooden posts.

"Maybe we could, y'know, catapult ourselves across the lake or something," he said, twanging the rope as he tightened it. Snookums was nipping at his ankles.

"Clear off, pooch!" snapped Grunt,

pushing Snookums out from under his feet.

No one was quite sure what happened next, whether Grunt got Snookums tangled up with the elastic rope or what, but one thing everyone was certain about: there was a "yap" from Snookums, a "grunt" from Grunt, a loud "twang" from the elastic rope and Snookums shot up and out over Shark Lake.

"SNOOKUMS!" squealed Sergeant Bones as he spotted his poodle flying overhead.

Snookums dropped with a splash right into the dead centre of Shark Lake.

"NOOOOOOOOO!" yelled Sergeant Bones. Within seconds, eight or nine dark fins circled Snookums, who yapped once and then went under followed quickly by the sharks. Sergeant Bones screamed like a six-year-old girl and leaped straight into the lake. "HOLD ON BABY, DADDY'S COMING!"

He dived under the surface and disappeared from view.

CHAPTER EIGHT

OOPS...

For a few seconds the Stunt Monkeys
stood frozen to the spot.

"Oops," said Grunt.

"Sarge?" said Kurtis in a quiet
voice. "You OK, Sarge?"

"We're doomed!" wailed Einstein.
"If Bones dies in there he'll kill us
for sure!"

Silence.

The lake was a mirror. Not the smallest ripple disturbed the surface.

Suddenly, about fifty metres away, the water erupted as Sergeant Bones leaped clear, holding Snookums in one hand and beating off a couple of sharks with the other.

"HEEEEEEEEEEEEEEEEEEEELLLLLLL LLLLLLLLLPPPPPPP!" he screeched before splashing back into the lake.

Kurtis raised an eyebrow.

"Now there's something you don't see everyday." He nodded towards the others and then at the lake. "Shall we?"

The Stunt Monkeys sprang into action, their record-breaking training clicking into place like a well-oiled machine. Leaping into the rowing boat, Grunt hung Stench over the stern, his butt dangling in the water. Einstein slipped his specially designed anti-glare specs on and took up a position as lookout at the front of the boat.

"Get farting, Stenchy!" shouted
Grunt. "Fart like you've never farted
before!"

Stench screwed his face up and
the boat lurched forward on a
powerful surge of butt-power.

"There!" shouted Einstein
pointing to his right, his
glasses revealing a dark
shape under the surface.
"There he blows!"

Sure enough,
after a moment,
Sergeant Bones popped up
spluttering and choking right where
Eisntein had pointed. Eight or nine
fins were circling him and Snookums
in a very menacing way indeed.

"Step on it, Stench!" snapped Kurtis as Stench turned the boat towards the Sergeant. "They haven't got much time!"

"He cannae get more power, Cap'n!" yelled Grunt. "We're at fart speed ten already!"

The boat was still about ten metres away from the Sergeant and Snookums when the sharks moved in to finish the job. Instantly Kurtis leaped from the boat and, using the sharks' backs as stepping stones, bounced nimbly across to Bones.

"SAVE SNOOKUMS!!" squeaked
the Sergeant, throwing the soaking
wet poodle towards Kurtis.
"CAREFUL, HE'S VERY SLIPPERY!"

Kurtis, used to handling
margarine-coated penguins, caught
Snookums expertly, spun on his heel
and hopped back to the boat, shark
nose by shark nose as they snapped
at his feet.

"SARGE!" yelled Einstein as Bones sank below the water one more time.

Kurtis turned away. "Don't look, Snookums," he said, covering the dog's eyes. "He's gone."

"GNNNNNAAAARRRGGGGHHH!" yelled Grunt as he sprinted to the front of the boat and dived straight in. "No one's going anywhere!" he yelled in mid-air. "Not on my watch!" He went under in a mighty splash and the water closed over him.

A few ripples, a bubble or two and then ... nothing.

"GRUNT!" yelled Stench, surprising everyone. "NOOOOOOOOOOOO!" Then he too dived overboard.

Horrified, Kurtis and Einstein watched and waited.

And waited.

Just as they had given up all hope, there was an explosion from behind them and Stench, farting like a kid possessed, surged clear of the lake in a roar of bubbles and foam, Grunt sitting on his shoulders. In one hand Grunt had hold of Sergeant Bones and was dragging him clear of the water. In the other he held the tails of nine sharks tied in a tight knot.

They thrashed and snapped at each
other as Grunt whirled them round
his head and threw them far out
across the lake.

"Whoo-ee!" he whooped. "Is this
the new World Record For Team

Speed Shark Rodeo or what?"

"Got to be!" yelled Kurtis as they all landed back at the jetty. "Too bad we don't have an official witness from The League Of Unbelievable and Amazing World Records!"

"Congratulations!" said Miss Axelsen from **The League Of Unbelievable and Amazing World Records**, stepping from her car. "I just happened to be passing on my way to Grotburg and saw the whole thing! You are now the holders of the **World Record For Team Speed Shark Rodeo!**"

"What an incredible coincidence, you being here to see it all!" said Grunt, picking a shark's tooth from his sock.

"I know!" said Miss Axelsen. "It's amazing, unbelievable!"

She shook hands with the Stunt Monkeys and gave them an official **League of Unbelievable and Amazing World Records** certificate.

"Keep up the good work, boys!" she said, as she got back in her car and whizzed off back to Grotburg.

On the jetty Sergeant Bones was coughing the last of the Shark Lake water out of his lungs. He had tight hold of Snookums.

The League of Unbelievable and Amazing World Records

Team Speed Shark Rodeo
The Stunt Monkeys

"THANKS, BOYS!" he screeched. "COUGH. YOU SAVED SNOOKUMS! HOW CAN I EVER, COUGH, REPAY YOU-AH?"

Kurtis stepped forward.

"Don't worry, Sarge. We'll think of something."

CHAPTER NINE

SLUDGEFEST HERE WE COME!

It was the morning of SludgeFest 50 and Mayor McFoodle wanted everything to be perfect.

"I want everything to be perfect, Pink!" he barked as they inspected the stage at Sludgeville Arena. "Nothing must go wrong. Nothing, I tell you! I don't want to look like a

fool in front of the Grand
Sludgemaster!"

"Of course not, Your Most
Graciousness," said Pink. "Everything
has been planned down to the very
last detail."

And so far things did indeed look
tickety-boo. Sludgeville was ready
for SludgeFest 50.

Not a single rule-breaker in sight.
Even the grass was behaving itself.
Everything was perfect, quiet,
orderly. A Sludgeville without the
Stunt Monkeys.

Which reminded Mayor McFoodle
– he needed to check something.

"Those damn Stunt Monkeys? Are
they taken care of?"

Pink paused and checked his clipboard.

"Yes, all tickety-boo, Your Honour. But are you sure we shouldn't have made them stay another day at Boot Camp? Just to be on the safe side?" Mayor McFoodle waved a chubby hand. "Do not be alarmed, Pink," he said. "I am confident that a month at Sergeant Bones's establishment will have completely knocked the stuffing out of those four hooligans. Besides, they're going to have much more

important things to think of today!
Remember that little matter of the
Princess SludgeFests? I don't think
those nasty little Stunt Monkeys are
going to cause any trouble
whatsoever!"

"In any event, Your Majesticness,"
said Pink. "I think they may have
learnt their lesson after all. Look,
there they are, already sitting in their
seats, quiet as mice."

Mayor McFoodle looked towards
the back of the arena where, just as
Pink had said, the Stunt Monkeys sat
quietly in their sparkly dresses
waiting for SludgeFest 50 to begin,
the big figure of Sergeant Bones
keeping a watchful eye on them.

"Capital, Pink!" said Mayor
McFoodle. "Capital!"

The sound of singing drifted
across Sludgeville Arena as the
Sludgeville Choir practised for the
big moment when the Grand
Sludgemaster would declare
SludgeFest 50 open.

"All you need is sludge, sludge! Sludge is all you need..."

Mayor McFoodle tapped his toe to the music and beamed. "It's going to be perfect, it is, it is!"

Up on Sludgeville Hill, Kurtis was looking through a pair of binoculars. SludgeFest 50 was due to start very soon.

"It's filling up. Not many empty seats now."

"What about us?" said Einstein. "How do we look?"

Kurtis swivelled round to check on the row of showroom dummies painted to look like the Stunt Monkeys

who sat motionless at the back of the arena. The dummy of Sergeant Bones had been padded out with cushions to make it more lifelike.

"We look great," said Kurtis, "very sparkly! McFoodle doesn't suspect a thing!"

"Are we nearly ready?" yelled Einstein, looking up at the top of the hill where Grunt and Sergeant Bones were hauling up the long elastic rope they'd borrowed from Boot Camp.

"Almost there!" shouted Grunt.

"JUST NEEDS TO BE FASTENED!" screamed Sergeant Bones.

The Stunt Monkeys were looking forward to SludgeFest 50 almost as much as Mayor McFoodle, although for very different reasons.

This was the Big One, the pay-off for all those spoiled World Records. The whole of Sludgeville was going to see the Stunt Monkeys perform the very first attempt at...

...The World Record For Elastic-Propelled Synchronized Flying Elvises!

Sergeant Bones looped the elastic rope around the back of the public toilets on Sludgeville Hill and gave the thumbs up to Grunt.

"Thanks, Sarge," said Grunt.

"THE LEAST AH COULD DO AFTER Y'ALL SAVED SNOOKUMS 'N' ME!" screamed Sergeant Bones.

The ends of the elastic rope were lashed to the top of the sludge storage towers about fifty metres away. The whole thing looked like a giant catapult.

Which is exactly what it was.

Down in Sludgeville Arena, Mayor McFoodle stood smiling as his Very Important guests arrived for the festival. Mrs McFoodle, in her best pink dress and fancy hat, posed for photographs. Horace, back from his balloon flight, stood next to her, picking his nose. "Nice big smile, Mrs McFoodle, if you please," said the photographer from *The Daily Sludge*.

"Lovely to see you," said Mayor McFoodle, shaking hands with the President of the Sludge Checkers Union.

"So pleased you could make it," he said to the wife of the boss of Sludge Industries.

"Everything is going brilliantly!" whispered Mayor McFoodle to Pink.

134

"Yes, Your Magnificence," said Pink. "All thanks to you, you are so, so clever! And look, here comes the Grand Sludgemaster himself!"

The Grand Sludgemaster grasped Mayor McFoodle's hand in a meaty paw and shook it hard.

"Hope this little shindig goes smoothly, McFoodle," he boomed. "You know how much I like things to go smoothly. The good name of sludge is in your hands today!"

"Of – of course Sludge Grandmaster
– Gludge Sandmaster – I mean
Grand Sludgemaster," stammered
Mayor McFoodle. "Absolutely nothing
will go wrong. You have my word!"

"See that it doesn't McFoodle, see
that it doesn't!"

The Grand Sludgemaster
lumbered off to his seat, his red
velvet robes swishing along the floor
– which reminded Mayor McFoodle
of something.

"The Sludge Princesses," said the
Mayor. "Get those Stunt Monkey
idiots down here right away, Pink!"

Back in the arena, the choir
started up with a rousing chorus of
"Sludgemakers Of The World Unite"
and SludgeFest 50 was under way!

The crowd clapped.

The real Stunt Monkeys watched
from up on the hill as the fake Stunt
Monkeys sat grinning at the stage,
their sparkly dresses glinting under
the lights.

Everything was ready.

The Grand Sludgemaster got to his feet and tapped the microphone.

"Ladies and gentlemen, boys and girls, Honourable Members of the Loyal Order of Sludgemasters," said the Grand Sludgemaster. "I'm very proud to have been asked here today to open the fiftieth SludgeFest because..."

Up on Sludgeville Hill, Stench held up his watch. "Parp!" he beeped, pointing to the dial.

"Let's go!" said Einstein.

The catapult was stretched to breaking point. The Stunt Monkeys put on their crash helmets, flexed

their white, rhinestone-studded Elvis
flight suits with the fold-out wings
(designed by Einstein and carefully
sewn in by Sergeant Bones), and
took their positions at the centre of
the gigantic catapult.

"Eagle One cleared for take-off!" yelled Grunt, adjusting his belt buckle.

"OK, boys," said Kurtis. "Let's rock and roll! Put the pedal to the metal!" He reached behind the catapult with a small penknife, but before he could cut the rope holding the catapult back, there was a horrible grinding noise and the entire toilet block, the Flying Stunt Monkey Elvises and a big chunk of the ground ripped free with an almighty PEEEOOOOIIIIIIINNNNGGGGGG!

"Uh-oh," said Kurtis as they flew upwards. "That's not good."

Down below, the Grand Sludgemaster was just getting into his stride. Behind him on the podium Mayor McFoodle smiled from ear to ear. This was great! He, Horace T. McFoodle, had pulled it off. It was an absolute triumph, no question about it! Perhaps he'd get the Grand Order of Loyal Sludgemasters medal! It was no more than he'd des—

Mayor McFoodle snapped out of his daydream. Someone was calling his name.

"McFoodle! McFoodle!"

"Yes, Grand Sludgemaster?" said

Mayor McFoodle.

The Grand Sludgemaster pointed at the sky.

"Is this part of the festival? Hmm?"

Mayor McFoodle looked up. Above him, hurtling towards the stage at a sickening speed – no, it was impossible surely – were four flying Elvises ... followed by what looked like an entire public toilet. A high-pitched scream came from inside the toilet block where Mrs Oona Conkdongler had, until a few seconds before, been enjoying a private moment.

"Yee-hah!" yelped Grunt as they passed over the roof of Sludgeville Arena.

"Parp!" farted Stench.

"Good grief," gulped Einstein.

"Waaaaaaaaaaaaaaaaaaaaaaaaaaa aaaaahhh!!!!" screamed Oona Conkdongler.

"Marvellous!" trilled Miss Axelsen from **The League Of Unbelievable and Amazing World Records**, sitting in the press box. She scribbled furiously in her notebook.

Up on the podium all was pandemonium. The TV cameras swung round to capture the Flying Elvises.

"McFoodle!" shouted the Grand Sludgemaster. "There are four Elvises and what looks like a public toilet heading towards us!"

Mayor McFoodle squirmed, trying to think of something to say. He needn't have worried because the very next second the Elvises, closely followed by the toilet block, bounced smack on to the canvas roof of the podium, and everything turned Very Nasty Indeed.

Amazingly, the Stunt Monkeys were thrown clear and landed safely

on a large pile of cardboard boxes. Mrs Oona Conkdongler flew clear of the impact, and would have smashed straight into the ground if it hadn't been for her large red and pink spotted knickers which acted like a parachute. She drifted safely to the ground, unharmed but extremely embarrassed.

The Grand Sludgemaster was not so lucky. A toilet landed square on his large head and knocked him off the podium. "McFOODLE!" he yelled, his voice echoing from inside the pan. "You won't hear the end of this!"

"Horace!" screamed Mayor McFoodle's mother from the VIP box.

"Mummy!" screamed Mayor McFoodle and fainted.

At the back of the arena, the Stunt Monkeys sat and watched.

"This is just great," said Einstein, eyeing Grunt. "Look what you did, you idiot! And poor Mrs Conkdongler! You should have known that toilet block wouldn't take the pressure!"

"Me?" said Grunt. "You were part of all this too, remember! And weren't you supposed to check the toilets were empty?"

"Never mind all that," said Kurtis. "Look over there. Things are about to get a whole lot worse."

"Worse?" yelled Grunt. "How could things possibly get any worse?"

Kurtis pointed at the sludge storage towers. Loosened by the force of the catapult they slowly toppled over. With a hideous roar a river of sludge poured down the hill … straight into the arena.

Raw sludge, as smelly as a river full of garlic-chewing skunks, slopped over the entire SludgeFest 50

site, covering the Grand
Sludgemaster, Mayor McFoodle,
Assistant Pink, the Ninja Traffic
Wardens, the Grass Inspectors and
all the VIPs, in no time at all. The
last the Stunt Monkeys saw of
Mayor McFoodle was him shouting
rude words as he sank below
the gunge.

A Sludge Industries advertising board floated towards the Stunt Monkeys and Kurtis jumped on it.

"C'mon," he said. "Let's get out of here."

Grunt, Einstein and Stench clambered aboard.

"How are we going to steer?" said Einstein. "We haven't got a paddle."

Stench dipped his butt in the sludge and began farting. The advertising board rose up on a bow wave and zipped away from the ruins of SludgeFest 50 into Sludge Creek.

"Paddle?" said Kurtis as they made their escape. "Who needs a paddle?"

DON'T MISS THE STUNT MONKEYS' NEXT AMAZING ADVENTURE!

MORE LOOPY STUNTS!

Rocket-propelled golf carts!

Inflatable suits!
Mayor McFoodle finally flips his lid!
...And it's all live on Stunt TV!

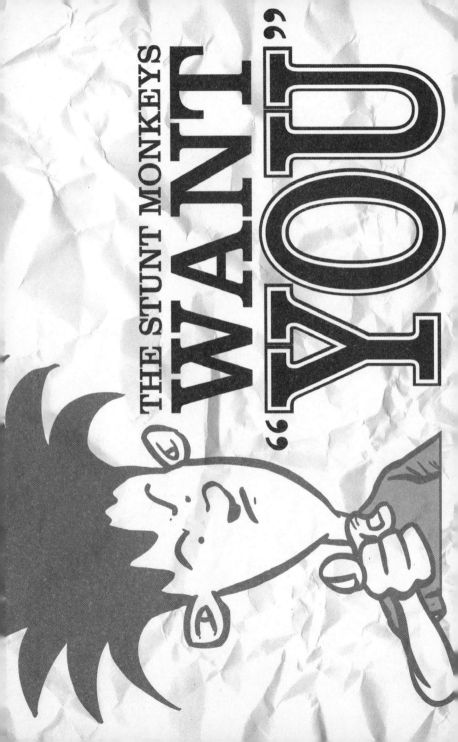

Are you up for anything?

Do you often find yourself thinking,

"I wonder what would happen if I shoved an entire packet of marshmallows in my mouth and then bounced on a trampoline"?

Have you got what it takes to monkey around?

If you answered "yes" to these questions and you've got a taste for stupidity and all-round, flat-out idiocy then the Stunt Monkeys need you … NOW!

Sign up right away for an exciting life!

Travel the world pushing peas up a path with your posterior!

Meet exciting people from all walks of life … and ask them to cram inside a phone booth with you!

We're not going to lie to you. It's a tough life in the Stunt Monkeys. Basic training can be hell and many won't make it.

But if you think you've got what it takes to be the best of the best, then sling in an application form at your Idiot Recruitment Office now!